TWISTAPLOT ™

6

CRASH LANDING!

Arthur Roth

ILLUSTRATIONS BY DAVID FEBLAND

SCHOLASTIC INC.
New York Toronto London Auckland Sydney Tokyo

ISBN 0-590-32726-7

Copyright © 1983 by Arthur Roth. All rights reserved. Published by Scholastic Book Services, a division of Scholastic Inc.

12 11 10 9 8 7 6 5 4 3 2 1   5   3 4 5 6 7/8

BEWARE!!!
DO NOT READ THIS BOOK FROM BEGINNING TO END

Your plane is about to make an unscheduled landing — a crash landing! In the short time you have left, you must decide whether to bail out in a parachute or take your chances by staying on board. And even if you reach the mountains or the endless desert in one piece, how will you find your way back to civilization?

Savage tribes, dangerous animals, impassable rivers, and unexplored jungles await you if you go one way. If you head in another direction, you may die of thirst or heatstroke in a scorching desert. Or, if you get lucky, you may find a fortune in buried treasure!

You will decide how to survive the terrors that await you by following the directions at the bottom of each page. If you choose wisely, safety — and maybe even fame and fortune — can be yours. Make the wrong decision, and you may spend the rest of your life in an unmapped jungle, far away from everything you know.

Your flight is now boarding on PAGE 2.

2

You are in a plane, flying over the Andes Mountains of South America, heading home after a week in Argentina. The trip you won for taking first place on the balance beam in your state's annual gymnastics competition was fun, but now you're eager to see your family again — Mom, Dad, your brother Tim, and your sister Cristina. You can hardly wait to tell them and your friends about your adventures. Although you had a wonderful time, you're a little homesick. You even miss your dog Flash and your pet hamster Miss Piggy. Thinking about missing things, you wonder how much work you missed in school. After a week in South America, your Spanish is improved, at least.

Suddenly the plane begins to bounce around. Your mouth goes dry, and you grip the arms of the seat. What is going on? Looking out the window, you realize that the plane is in a blinding storm. Lightning flashes, and you shrink back into your seat. The plane gives a sickening lurch, and someone screams. You feel like screaming, too, but instead you clap your hand over your mouth. Just then you hear a shout and look up. A steward named Wayne is standing at the head of the aisle.

Go on to PAGE 3.

"I must have your attention!" he orders.

Everyone calms down for a second. You strain forward to hear better. The plane bumps in the air.

"We've lost an engine, and the plane is losing altitude," Wayne announces. "The captain will have to crash-land the plane. As it happens, we have a dozen parachutes on board that we were delivering for the Air Force. The captain would like volunteers to use the parachutes. The less weight there is on the plane, the longer he will be able to keep it airborne, and the more time he'll have to find a safe landing place."

You're not sure what to do. Jumping with a parachute could be dangerous, but crash-landing a plane is dangerous, too. You haven't got much time to decide.

Across the aisle, Gloria and Jeff, two young people you met at the airport, volunteer to jump.

"I'm not sure what to do," you tell them. "I'm scared to jump, and I'm scared to stay on the plane." You've got to decide — fast!

Go on to PAGE 4.

4

You notice that several of the younger (and stronger) passengers have volunteered to jump. You think your chances of survival are better if you stick with them. On the other hand, the older passengers, who have decided to stay on the plane, have a much wider experience of life.

"What are the jumpers' chances?" you ask Wayne.

"Pretty good," he says. "The jumpers will probably land without getting hurt, but they will have to hike out. Crash-landing with the plane is more dangerous, but your chances of being rescued are better, because it's easier for search parties to find a plane than a person."

"What are you going to do?" you ask Wayne.

"I'm going with the jumpers," Wayne says. "I've had survival training, so I can be useful to them."

Already Wayne is strapping a middle-aged man into a chute. A young girl is in the doorway, getting ready to jump. It's now or never. You groan. Your first time away from home on your own, and look what's happening. You don't have anyone to help you make the most important decision of your life!

If you decide to jump, turn to PAGE 6.

If you decide to stay on board, turn to PAGE 12.

You are the last one to jump out of the plane, except for Wayne. It is not too late to change your mind.

"Remember, count to ten, then pull this handle," Wayne says. "Let's go!" Suddenly you are falling! You almost forget to count, then remember and start with *four*. At ten you pull the handle. A sudden jerk, and you are floating down. What a relief! You pull on the riser cords and find that you can guide your chute. Far below you, the other chutes are floating toward a snow-covered peak. Three go down on the near side, while two others go drifting past on the opposite side.

Which group should you follow? You have to decide soon. At the foot of the peak on this side, there is a vast jungle with a river flowing through it. On the other side, you catch a glimpse of endless desert.

The jungle side will be dangerous, but you should find food and water there. However, your chances of being spotted by a search plane are greater in the open desert than in the tree-covered jungle. It's hunger and thirst — against wild animals and snakes. You count the riser cords, naming one cord *jungle* and the next cord *desert*.

If you guess that the last cord comes up jungle, turn to PAGE 9.

If you guess that the last cord comes up desert, turn to PAGE 7.

You keep in view the pair of parachutes drifting down toward the desert. The peak slides past; you are below it now. Soon the desert ground is rushing up fast. You hit, tumble end over end, and come to a sudden stop. Someone has hurled himself on your billowing chute, collapsing it. You struggle out of the harness and find yourself facing a young woman and a middle-aged man with a big, bushy beard. "You made it," the man says. "I'm Pierre, and this is Maria Duran."

You give them your name.

"How many finally jumped?" Pierre asks.

"I think about six," you say.

"I wonder where the others are?" Maria says.

"Some went down on the jungle side of that big mountain we drifted past," you say.

"And Wayne?" Pierre asks.

"He jumped after me," you say. "I don't know where he landed."

"Well, before we do anything, let's check if we have any food or water," Pierre suggests.

In your rush to leave the plane, you left everything behind. Darn! Maria shakes her head. She has nothing, either.

Go on to PAGE 8.

8

"All I have is a bag of M&M's I found in my pocket," Pierre says. "We will divide them evenly." He opens the bag and starts to count them out. There are forty-five. You take your fifteen and put them away in an inside pocket. Maria takes her fifteen and pockets them, too. Pierre puts his away, then he looks up at the sun. "We have a choice," he says. "Head south for the Amazon River, or east for the Atlantic coast."

"Which is closer?" you ask.

"I have no idea," Pierre says.

Pierre takes an M&M out of his pocket and hides it in his fist. "Orange — we go for the Amazon. Brown — we go for the Atlantic," he says. "Choose!"

You feel confused. Why is he rushing you? "Wait a minute," you say. "Maybe we should try to go back the way we came and look for the others."

"Well, we have to do something," Pierre says. "We just can't sit here."

"If we stay here, rescue planes will be out looking for us," you argue. "If we just wander around, we'll exhaust ourselves before they can find us. What do you think, Maria?"

"I'm for moving on," Maria says.

"Choose!" Pierre insists. "Orange for the Amazon, brown for the Atlantic."

If you guess brown, turn to PAGE 10.
If you guess orange, turn to PAGE 28.

You spot two figures on a rocky shelf on the jungle side of the mountain. You guide your chute over to Jeff and Gloria. A minute later Wayne comes down.

At one end of the rock shelf there is a steep icefield that drops away for hundreds of feet. If you lose your footing, you will be dashed to death on the piled-up rocks below. At the other end of the ledge there is a sheer drop-off of thirty feet down to another narrow ledge.

"We'll have to go down the icefield," Wayne says.

"No," Jeff says. "We can cut our riser cords and make a rope long enough to reach the ledge below us."

"We should all stick together," you remind everyone.

"I don't care what you guys do," Jeff argues. "I'm a mountain climber, and I'm going down to the ledge."

You feel there is greater safety with two people, Jeff and Gloria, instead of just one, Wayne. But Wayne is older and more confident and is supposed to have had survival training. Also, Jeff is too cocky. He has no idea of what might await you on the lower ledge.

If you go down the icefield with Wayne, turn to PAGE 47.

If you go to the ledge with Jeff and Gloria, turn to PAGE 15.

You trudge onward with Maria and Pierre, heading for the Atlantic coast. You hope you have made the right decision.

The air gets hotter and hotter, and finally you are all forced to seek shelter under a bush. You wonder if you have done the right thing by jumping. If you had stayed on the plane, you might have been rescued by now.

Maria and Pierre carefully eat their M&M's one by one. Just watching them makes you hungry. You eat all of yours at once, just the way you do at home, forgetting that you should hoard them. They taste great, and right now you just don't care.

A storm begins to build up. Bolts of lightning flash, and claps of thunder rattle across the skies.

The chocolate and sugar from the candy have given you some energy. "I'll go see if we can find a better place to shelter," you tell Pierre and Maria. "Maybe those bluffs in the distance will protect us from the storm."

Pierre and Maria decide you should all stay together, so they set off with you. As you approach the bluffs, Maria spots a cave halfway up the cliff. The lightning is flashing around the open ground where you are standing, when off in the distance, you spot a tall plume of dust rising to the sky.

Go on to PAGE 11.

"Maybe it's a convoy of trucks," you say hopefully.

Pierre disagrees. "It's probably a desert whirlwind. Just forget it, and let's go up to that cave before it starts raining."

The lightning flashes awfully close to you, but you'd still like to check out that tall dust plume. It could be your only chance to be rescued.

You don't know what to do. Something tells you that the dust cloud means people. On the other hand, you don't want to stay out in the open desert during the middle of an electrical storm. Plus, you know you ought to stick with Pierre and Maria. What should you do?

If you follow the others to the cliff, turn to PAGE 13.

If you head for the plume of dust, turn to PAGE 25.

You check your seatbelt, then look around the plane. You hope you have made the right decision — to stay on board. Suddenly you notice trees rushing by the side window. Here it comes!

Kerrump! The plane hits. You are aware of tumbling over and over. You see blue sky just ahead of you. Somehow the plane has broken in two. You can't believe it, but you are still alive and unhurt. You come to rest, still strapped into your seat. The rest of the plane is nowhere to be seen. You examine yourself. Nothing seems to be broken. However, you can't get out of your seat because the seatbelt is jammed. You wonder if you should just sit there and wait until someone finds you. Or should you sort of half-jump, half-hop in your seat and try to follow the bits and pieces of wreckage, hoping they will lead you to the main body of the plane?

If you're the kind of person who always buckles your seatbelt, turn to PAGE 23.

If you never buckle up, guess what? Your plane ride has reached

THE END

You, Pierre, and Maria reach the bottom of the cliff. On a ledge, about forty feet up, is the cave, large enough to hold everyone. There is a big crack in the rock face, and you start to climb up. This is where your training as a gymnast pays off. You keep inside the crack as much as possible, jamming your body into the opening. You move up, using friction, one foot jammed against one edge of the crack, the other foot doubled back and jammed against the opposite edge. Just before you reach the ledge, your way is blocked by a large boulder jammed in the crack. No matter how you twist or turn, you can't climb around or above it.

There is one chance. If Pierre can follow you up the crack and then climb onto your shoulders, he should be able to reach the ledge. Once up there, he can lie down and pull you and Maria up.

"Come on, you can do it!" you yell at Pierre. "If I can do it, you can." After all, he is a big, strong man. Why would he be afraid? "Well, are you coming?" you shout down. "I can't wait here all day."

He still hesitates, reminding you of some of your friends who, when the going gets tough, go right home.

If Pierre reminds you of any of your friends, turn to PAGE 22.

If Pierre doesn't remind you of anyone, turn to PAGE 14.

Pierre climbs up on your shoulders and pulls himself up on the ledge. Next, Maria climbs up and reaches safety, too. Then Pierre pulls you up. Just in time, too, as lightning flashes all around the cliff face. You rush into the cave to take shelter.

After a while the storm eases up.

"Let's climb down," you say. "There's still an hour or two of daylight left."

"I think we ought to stay here for the night," Pierre argues. "We can get a good rest and be fresh in the morning."

"It's more important to keep moving," you say. "Maybe planes are out looking for us right now. They'll never spot us hidden in the cave."

"You're right," Maria says.

"The storm isn't over yet," Pierre argues. "There is still an occasional flash of lightning."

If you usually go to bed before 9:30, snuggle up on PAGE 17.

If you usually go to bed after 9:30, climb down to PAGE 18.

Jeff has finished making a rope out of the riser cords, and he fastens it to a rocky knob. He shows you and Gloria how to go down on the rope in a mountaineer's rappel.

Jeff looks down over the edge. "There's a spike of rock sticking out from the cliff about sixty feet down," he says. He lets down the doubled rope, but both ends fall six feet short. "It won't reach all the way," he says. "Whoever goes first—when you reach the end of the rope, you have to fall free the last six feet and land on the spike. Then you can reach up to help the others."

"Okay, I'll go," you finally say. You start down, reach the end of the doubled rope, and look down. If you miss that spike, you'll fall another fifty feet. For a moment you panic. You are gripping the rope so tightly your knuckles are white.

"Geronimo!" you scream, and drop. At the last moment your legs straddle the spike. You turn around to face the cliff. You help Gloria, then Jeff, to come down. Another fifty-foot rappel off the spike, and you reach a long slope. Jeff and Gloria start down, and you lose sight of them, but the way is clear enough.

Go on to PAGE 16.

"We're over here!" Jeff calls. "We all made it!"

You notice that Gloria is sitting down. "What happened?" you ask.

"Sprained my ankle," Gloria says.

"One of us will have to stay with her," Jeff says, "and the other one go for help."

"Gloria, you decide who goes and who stays," you say.

If you think Gloria wants you to stay, turn to PAGE 20.

If you think Gloria wants you to go for help, turn to PAGE 32.

You stay in the cave. It grows dark, and you all drift off to sleep. In the middle of the night a crashing noise wakes you up out of a nightmare. You dreamed that a landslide from the bluff covered up the mouth of your cave. You give a shiver. What a nightmare, to be trapped in the cave forever! In a little while you go back to sleep.

Hours later you wake up. It is still dark, but you seem to have slept a long time.

"Pierre? Maria?" you call out.

"Yes?" Pierre says.

"Isn't it morning yet?" you ask.

"Why is it still so dark?" Maria says.

You hear Pierre moving around. "I can't find the mouth of the cave!" Pierre says.

Then you realize that the landslide was no dream. That crashing noise you heard was an avalanche of rocks and mud coming down and covering the mouth of the cave. You walk to the back of the cave. Perhaps there is another way out. You bump into rock. You keep patting here and there, hoping to find an opening.

Finally you sink to your knees, defeated. Soon all that is heard is a small, weak voice saying over and over again, "Is there anyone out there?"

There isn't, and this really is

THE END

You talk Pierre and Maria into going back down the cliff. But then you discover that some things are possible to climb up, but can't be climbed down.

You try all sorts of movements: you holding Maria by the wrists; Pierre holding you by the ankles; you holding Pierre. Nothing works; you can't get back into the crack that leads down to the foot of the cliff.

Suddenly you hear a whirring noise in the sky. A helicopter! You dance around on the ledge and wave your arms. The pilot spots you, brings his craft in close to the face of the cliff, and lets down a steel cable with a basket chair dangling from it. Maria steps in and is lifted off to safety. Next it's Pierre's turn and he, too, is rescued. Soon you are plucked from the ledge, and the three of you are headed for civilization — safe at last!

THE END

You and Gloria stay behind and watch Jeff march off. Then you set about making a comfortable place for Gloria to lie down and rest her sprained ankle. You rip branches off trees and manage to make a shelter. Then there is nothing to do but wait for Jeff to return.

"If we only had a pack of cards," Gloria says.

"If we only had a color TV set," you say.

"If we only had some apple pie, we could have apple pie and ice cream, if we only had some ice cream," Gloria says.

That cracks you up, and you start laughing. For half an hour you both play "if onlys," but it gets boring. Then you remember a game that you and your sister Cristina used to play.

"Tell you what," you say. "I bet I can think up worse curses than you can."

"Bet you can't," Gloria says.

"May you wake up in the morning with a wart the size of a potato in the middle of your forehead," you say.

"May you fall on your back so hard it breaks your nose," Gloria says.

"May you have fleas as big as roosters, as busy as bees, and as hungry as bears." You are really getting warmed up now.

Go on to PAGE 21.

"May you live like an onion," Gloria says, "with your head in the ground and your legs in the air."

"May you live like a light fixture," you reply, "hanging by day and burning by night."

Your cursing competition is interrupted by the sound of men and horses. Four riders are passing by about a hundred yards away. They are rough-looking, ominous characters.

What if they're bandits? You hesitate, even though this could be your big chance to get out of here.

"Should we follow them or not?" you whisper to Gloria.

"I don't know," Gloria says. "What do you think?"

If today's date is an odd number, follow the men to PAGE 27.

If today's date is an even number, go to PAGE 81 and stay put.

Pierre refuses to climb up, and you start back down the crack. You discover that climbing down is much harder than climbing up. But you slowly make progress and finally reach the foot of the cliff.

Pierre holds out a hand to help you down the last few steps. You jump and land beside him. He grabs your right arm to keep you from falling. Maria grabs your other arm. For a moment the three of you are joined together.

And at that exact moment there is a mighty flash of lightning, brighter than the light of a thousand suns. When the lightning strike is over, three puffs of smoke rise from the desert floor.

THE END

You stay where you are, strapped into your seat. You keep shouting, but no one answers. Meanwhile you work away on that jammed seatbelt. Finally it pops free! You get out of the seat and look around for the plane. The trail of leveled trees and pieces of wreckage is easy to follow.

Hours later you spot the plane, far below you. Then you see people moving around! You hurry toward the site, and soon you are greeted by the other survivors. You introduce yourself. The others are:

Spike Harris, treasure hunter.

Willy Killmore, U.S. Army General.

Jenny Jogalotto, 70-year-old running grandmother.

Dr. Arthur Drib, a bird-watcher.

Cliff Byte, computer expert.

"Let's get organized!" General Killmore shouts. "First we search the plane for food. Remember, every little bit counts."

Everyone goes through the wreckage. Jenny finds a salami sandwich. Dr. Drib finds a granola bar. Cliff doesn't even bother to get up to look. When everything is laid out, there is hardly enough for even one person.

"Okay," the General says. "We have to decide whether to stay with the plane, or hike out."

Go on to PAGE 24.

"Let's stay," Cliff says. For a young man, Cliff looks pretty out of shape, and just the thought of hiking makes him tired.

"If we stay, we'll have a place to take shelter," you point out.

"That's true," Cliff says. "Also search planes are more likely to find us."

"If we hike out, we'll soon be down to where it's warm," Jenny says. "Maybe we can find more food. There's none here."

"Let's take a vote," you suggest.

"No need," the General says. "Whoever wants to hike out can follow me, and I'll lead you to safety. Whoever wants to stay behind can do so."

If you want to follow the General, turn to PAGE 63.

If you want to stay behind, turn to PAGE 30.

You tell Maria and Pierre that you want to check out the dust plume. "It's only a mile or so away," you say.

"You can't tell," Pierre says. "It could be ten miles off."

"It's not a good idea to split up," Maria says.

You insist on making the detour. "Look," you say. "Let me check it out. If it's nothing, I can always come back and follow your tracks until I catch up."

"If it rains there won't be any tracks — you'll get lost," Pierre says, correctly. But you still feel you have to check out whatever is creating that dust. Besides, it seems to you that Pierre is too lazy, or too scared, to try any other plan. Finally you say goodbye, then start following a route that will intercept the dust cloud. The closer you get, the stranger the dust plume looks. Soon you hear a weird drumming sound. What is it?

What looked like a dust cloud is really a cloud of grasshoppers — a plague, millions of them! You sink to the ground, buried under tons of grasshoppers. Grasshoppers get in your mouth and ears and nose. Every time you breathe, you swallow three or four. Soon you have swallowed so many grasshoppers that, instead of walking, you hop! This is the end, you think.

Go on to PAGE 26.

The grasshopper cloud passes, and now you see another weird sight. Thousands of birds are following the grasshoppers, gobbling them up. Some birds have eaten so many grasshoppers they can't fly. All they can do is hop! You just hope there won't be an army of cats following the birds, and thousands of dogs following the army of cats.

Finally the grasshoppers hop off, the birds hop after them, and you are all hopped out. The desert is quiet again.

You think of returning to Pierre and Maria, but Pierre was right. You've lost all sense of direction and have no idea where they are. The sun gets hotter, and you collapse on the ground. Your eyes close, and you have difficulty breathing. Is this the end? Will you ever see your home again? Your mom and dad, your sister, your brother? Will you ever see the old gang at the Elm Tree Diner? You pass out.

You wake up in a hospital. An oil prospector discovered you and brought you to safety. He was attracted by the sight of vultures wheeling in the sky. Some of the vultures were already on the ground, hopping toward you. He got there just in time!

THE END

"I'll follow them," you say to Gloria, keeping an eye on the horsemen. "You stay here. If it seems safe, I'll lead them back to you. If not, I'll come back alone, okay?"

"Fine," Gloria agrees.

You follow the four horsemen. You notice each rider carries an upright lance with a triangular flag. As the first horseman passes by, on a red horse, you read the word on the flag: WAR. The second horse is white, and the flag reads: PESTILENCE. Wasn't that an ancient word for disease? The third horse is pale gray, and the rider's flag reads: DEATH. The fourth horse is black, and that flag reads: FAMINE.

The horsemen ride by, and you shrink back. You have just seen the Four Horsemen of the Apocalypse! You remember your social studies teacher saying that back in the Middle Ages people believed the Four Horsemen of the Apocalypse would ride back and forth across the land just before the end of the world.

When they are safely out of sight, you get to your feet and run as fast as you can back to Gloria. But when you reach her, you find that you have completely forgotten what the horsemen looked like. All you can say is, "The horsemen were evil. They could not help us."

Now turn to PAGE 81 to find out what happens to you and Gloria.

You fold up your parachute, tie it on your back, and head for the Amazon River with Pierre and Maria. The land is full of high thornbushes. You see no animals, no birds, not even insects. The sun is scorching. Finally Pierre says, "We have to stop and find shade. I'm too tired to go on."

Maria agrees with him. You argue with them. You think it's important to keep on the move while you're still fresh. You don't want to stop, but the other two insist. You give in, unfold your parachute, and snag one end on top of a bush, anchoring the other end to the ground with rocks. All three of you crawl underneath the makeshift tent.

"Were you going home when the plane ran into trouble?" Pierre asks.

You tell Pierre of your free vacation for winning the balance beam event in gymnastics.

"And you?" you ask.

"I was going to San Francisco to sign a business deal. I have invented a new product called E-Quil. It has no taste or color. E-Quil takes out half of the strongest flavor in any dish. Say your soup is too salty. One tablet of E-Quil draws out half the salt. You leave E-Quil in for a minute, then take it out, and your soup tastes delicious again. E-Quil works with pepper, garlic, anything."

Go on to PAGE 29.

"Sounds pretty good," you say, doubt-fully.

"Shouldn't we sleep now?" Maria asks.

"Good idea," Pierre agrees. "Maybe we can walk again at dusk, when it is much cooler."

Everyone goes to sleep.

An hour later you wake up. Off on the horizon you notice a peculiar shimmer in the air, like giant heat waves rising from the ground. You want to sneak away from the others and find out what it is. It looks like a rainbow, except that the bands are all the same color, a bright, vibrating, golden hue. You can hear faint strains of a tan-talizing, half-remembered tune that makes your fingers itch to have your guitar in your hands. Should you go? Or stay with the others until they wake up?

If you play a musical instrument, turn to PAGE 33.

If you don't play a musical instrument, turn to PAGE 43.

Cliff Harris wants to stay, and you join him. You can at least shelter yourself near the plane and hope that someone spots you. The others leave with the General.

"Now what?" Cliff asks.

"It's going to get cold," you say. "Let's gather all the clothes we can find. Then we'll start a fire to keep warm and attract rescuers."

You notice that Cliff stops work every couple of minutes to rest. Just watching him huffing and puffing makes you tired.

"Let's get some sleep," you say. "It's almost dark."

Go on to PAGE 31.

The next morning you wake up early and decide to leave Cliff asleep while you backtrack on the trail of wreckage. You find a suitcase with someone's lunch inside: two ham sandwiches, two celery sticks, and six Oreo cookies. You sit down and eat a ham sandwich.

Then you notice, far off, a straight line that could be a road. Should you head for the road instead of going back to Cliff? You don't really want to share your food with him. On the other hand, he is probably depending on you to see him through. It's a hard decision. You don't even have a coin to flip.

If you go back to Cliff, turn to PAGE 60.
If you take off on your own, turn to PAGE 36.

You hike off, leaving Jeff and Gloria behind. You walk through an evergreen forest in high mountain country until darkness forces you to stop. You curl up under the roots of a fallen tree and try to sleep.

It is cold and uncomfortable. You think of your room back home. A soft, warm bed. A stereo cassette player with earphones so that you can listen to your favorite music. A comforting night light in case you have to get up in the middle of the night. You start to feel very lonely. You suddenly feel so homesick you can hardly stand it.

Somewhere in the distance an owl hoots, and you shiver. Then the next thing you know, it's morning. You head downhill as best you can. At noon you run across a spring, where you take a long drink of water. Then you stretch out on the grass. The sun is warm; your eyes close, and you fall asleep.

When you wake up hours later, the shadows are very long. You notice a weird pinkish glow in the sky, as though part of the forest were on fire. Should you head for the glow?

If you head for the glow, turn to PAGE 35.

If you continue on your original course, turn to PAGE 41.

You start walking toward the glow. Hours later, the shimmering light seems no closer. You stagger up a hill to look around. Then you spot the Golden Arches—OVER 30 BILLION SOLD! You crawl toward that friendly place and finally reach the counter.

"One burger, a large fries, and a chocolate shake," you groan.

"Coming up!" the girl says.

You are so hungry you could eat the paper napkins.

"Here we are," the girl says. You reach for a delicious-looking French fry. Your fingers go right through the fries and out the other side! You grab at the hamburger, but your hand glides right on through.

"What's going on?" you shout.

"I'm sorry, sir," the girl says. "We're a mirage."

"A mirage!" you cry. "I want food!"

"Oh, sir, try to understand." She reaches out to pat you on the shoulder, but her hand goes right through your arm.

"I want food!" you shout. "Food! Food! Food! How can I get something to eat?" you demand.

The girl points to the rolling sandhills and the shimmering heat waves. "You can go back out there," she says. "Or you can join us and become part of the mirage."

"I want to go home," you protest.

Go on to PAGE 34.

"Cheer up. It's quite nice here," the girl says. "You can start out salting French fries, then work your way up. You play checkers?"

"Checkers?"

"We need someone for the checkers team."

You start banging the counter. Salting French fries and playing checkers—what a life! You've got to *do* something!

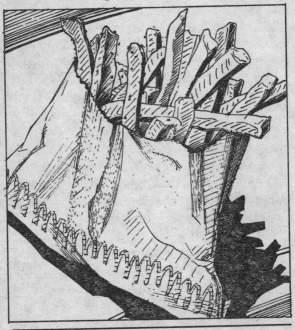

If you decide to return to the desert, turn to PAGE 39.

If you decide to stay at the mirage restaurant, turn to PAGE 38.

You head for the glow. Hours later you stumble across a rocky barrier of some sort. Somehow you climb over it. You come to a large tree and decide to spend the night there. The forest is spooky, and you are afraid of wild animals. You climb the tree and find a large, leafy nest in a fork.

During the night the roaring of an animal wakens you several times, and you are glad to be safe in the tree. When morning comes, you see a band of monkeys. Then a lion moving across a field. Next comes a giraffe. What's happening? This looks more like Africa than South America.

A man suddenly appears on a path, carrying an armful of loose hay. In the distance you notice houses, a church steeple, a water tower. Suddenly you realize that you have stumbled into the middle of a zoo on the outskirts of a large town. You are overjoyed! You tell the man about your friends, and that evening you are reunited with Jeff and Gloria, who have been rescued by some of the townspeople.

Jeff is so impressed by your successful mission that he asks you to join him later in the year on an expedition to climb Mount Everest. You tell him that you will think about it. In the meantime, you are all on your way home—safe at last!

THE END

You take the extra food and head off away from Cliff. By noon you have reached a stream. You drink some water and take a rest. That straight line still seems to be miles away. You think of poor Cliff. He is probably hungry, but he deserves it. He was too lazy to even help you look for food.

You hike all afternoon, through tangled woods and thorny bushes. Just about dark, you hear a strange, rumbling sound. Is it a truck coming along a road? You hurry up, pushing through undergrowth. The sound gets louder.

You burst through some bushes, just in time to see the back end of a railroad caboose drawing away from you. That straight line was a railroad. You shout and wave your arms, but the freight train pulls steadily away.

You collapse beside the tracks. You're exhausted. Should you just stay here until another train comes along?

If a train comes to your town, turn to PAGE 45.

If no train comes near where you live, you're on the wrong track! Go back to PAGE 1 and begin a new adventure.

You go to work salting French fries and playing on the checkers team. You're named Employee of the Month twice in a row and finally get promoted to counterman. Several days later your first stranger comes in from outside. He is an old man with a long white beard. He staggers to the counter and orders a burger and a Coke. He pulls out his wallet to pay and a Social Security card drops to the counter. You pick it up. It has your name and number. But how can that be? You stare at the stranger.

He looks familiar, as though he were your grandfather or someone like that. Then you notice a tiny, white, star-shaped scar on the back of his left hand. Why, you have a similar scar in the very same place!

You scream and turn away. The kitchen disappears. The light fades to a tiny white dot, as though the world were a TV set that had just been turned off. Then the white dot blinks out and your adventure has come to

THE END

The desert heat outside the mirage restaurant hits you like the blow of a fist. You crawl away, thinking how cool it was in there. You crawl all day and all night. You have no idea where you are. You're tired, hungry, and thirsty; yet you keep on crawling.

In the morning you see a strange sight. Ahead is a large four-engine plane. You give a hoarse cry. You are saved! It must be a rescue plane, but no one seems to be around. Maybe they are out searching for you.

You reach an open door in the side of the plane. You pull yourself up. Inside, two men are sitting in the nose of the plane, their backs to you. The pilot and copilot, you think, and call out, "Hey, you guys, can you help me? I'm in bad shape."

Silence. The men don't even turn around.

"Come on, give me a break, huh?" you plead.

You reach out and put one hand on the top of the pilot's helmet. The body falls forward with a dry rattling sound and rolls over. You look down at a clean white skull, framed inside a flying helmet. You cry out, then turn to the copilot. Another dry skull grins back at you. You turn away in horror. How long ago did the plane land? Months, at least.

Go on to PAGE 40.

You search everywhere, looking for food or water. All you find is an old newspaper with the headline, *Allied Armies Invade France!* You check the date. June 9, 1944.

Now you know the truth. The plane crashed in the desert almost forty years ago. In all that time you have been the only one to find it.

Then a horrible thought strikes you. How many years will it be before anyone else finds the plane—and a third skeleton?

THE END

You head into the forest, away from the pinkish glow. You find jungle fruit to eat, but it tastes sour; you're afraid it might be poisonous. You think of your mother's cooking and groan with hunger. A dish of creamy scrambled eggs, you think, and a tall glass of cold orange juice. Or maybe a steaming bowl of her spaghetti, with that special mushroom marinara sauce. You'd even go for her tuna fish casserole, your least favorite dish.

You walk all day and finally stumble across a river. You decide to follow it downstream. The banks are overgrown with bushes, so you decide to wade into the stream. Underwater branches cut your legs. The bleeding attracts piranha fish, and several times you leap to the bank where you yank half a dozen of these tiny killer fish off your legs. You make sure never to get too far away from shore when you are wading.

You are also attacked by leeches, big black slugs that weaken you by sucking your blood. *Yeeuch!*

Go on to PAGE 42.

Toward evening you spot two natives paddling a dugout canoe along the river. You call out, but they don't understand English. They motion for you to swim out to them.

You are afraid of the piranha fish. One drop of blood and the water will boil with a seething mass of these tiny killers. But you have no choice. Slowly you wade out. Soon you can feel a tickling all over your legs. The leeches are attacking you again. If they draw blood, it will attract the piranha fish, and it will be all over for you.

Halfway to the canoe you get an idea. You reach down and pull off half a dozen leeches. What you are going to do is disgusting, but it may save your life. One after another you bite the leeches in two, then throw both halves as far downstream as you can.

Instantly the piranha fish swim off and attack the new target. In minutes the feeding frenzy is over, and they head back to you. Luckily, you reach the canoe first. The two natives pull you aboard and bring you to the nearest settlement.

The next day an army patrol is sent out to pick up Jeff and Gloria. The three of you have a joyful reunion, and a week later you head back home, with a big appetite and an incredible story to tell your family and friends.

THE END

You go back to sleep. When you wake up, hours later, the shimmer on the horizon is gone. You no longer hear the music. You decide not to tell the others. Maybe you were seeing things. After all, strange things happen in the desert.

The three of you resume hiking. Now that the sun has set, it is much cooler. As you walk along, Pierre tells you more about his invention. "It will make me a fortune."

You don't really care that much about his invention and tune out. Instead you wonder what your folks and everybody at home will think when they hear your plane crashed. The kids in school will freak out. They won't know whether you're alive or dead.

In the meantime, you are stuck with Pierre and Maria. You probably made a mistake picking the desert pair to follow. Pierre doesn't seem that smart, and Maria isn't much better. Maybe you should split, you think. You have a feeling you could do much better on your own.

Fortunately, there is a full moon, so it is fairly easy to see where you are going. Finally Maria suggests stopping for a while. You all take a long rest. Soon the dawn breaks and the sky floods with light. Off to your left you see a tumbled pile of red walls; they look like the ruins of an old fort. You point them out to the others.

Go on to PAGE 44.

"No, those are just sandstone towers," Pierre says.

"Let's hike over there to make sure," you suggest.

"Are you crazy?" Pierre says. "That could be ten miles out of the way."

"I'm telling you it's an old fort," you argue. You're getting mad at Pierre. Why is he always wrong? You appeal to Maria.

"I don't know," Maria says. "It's hard to tell what they are."

"There would be a flag flying if it was a fort," Pierre argues. "I'll bet there's no one there."

"We might find food," you say. "Or even a well. We need water."

Your mouth is so dry your tongue feels like sandpaper. You want to go to the fort. Pierre wants to keep going south.

"You decide," you say to Maria.

Suddenly she covers her eyes. "Guess the color of my eyes," she says to you. "Guess right, and we go to the fort. Guess wrong, and we head south."

If your eyes are brown or hazel, head south to PAGE 62.

If your eyes are blue or gray, go to the fort on PAGE 46.

You settle down beside the tracks. It gets dark, and you fall asleep. You find yourself having a strange dream. You are riding an elephant and being chased by crooks in a car. Suddenly the gangsters are all on water skis, being towed by the elephant. One crook keeps shooting at you, but instead of a bullet, a Ping-Pong ball comes out of his gun. It plops into the water, where a cruising shark bounces it along with the tip of his nose.

This upsets the other crooks, who all scream, "No fair using floaties!"

What are floaties? you wonder. Suddenly the elephant stumbles. The ground is shaking. It's an earthquake! The dream is so real you wake up. But what's this? The ground really is shaking. A big white eye looms in the distance. Of course! It's a train!

But how do you stop it? Should you stand *between* the rails and wave your arms to get the engineer's attention, then jump aside at the last minute? Or should you stand *beside* them, and trust that the engineer will notice you if you're off to the side?

If you stand between the rails, turn to PAGE 50.

If you stand beside the rails, turn to PAGE 58.

You, Maria, and Pierre head for the tumbled walls of rock and find that it is an old deserted fort. You do not find any food or water. You toss aside an empty bottle someone left behind.

"Let's take a look around," you suggest.

The other two shake their heads. They are too tired. You decide to investigate a clump of bushes some distance away. Such green, healthy-looking growth might mean water nearby. An hour later you reach the spot. You poke around, forcing your way into the heart of the bushes. Suddenly the ground gives way, and you are falling!

"Help!" you scream.

Kerrump! You hit bottom. For a moment you are stunned. High above, you see a round hole and blue sky. You touch the rocky sides of the hole and realize you have fallen into an old, dried-up well. A ray of sunshine lights up a piece of metal. You touch it, then scrape away some moss, and discover a wooden door. You get all excited. Maybe there is food inside! The metal is a lock — and the key is in it!

If you never lose your housekey, turn to PAGE 49.

If you can never find your housekey, turn to PAGE 59.

Don't have a housekey? Then you're locked out of the rest of this adventure! Close the book, then start again.

Jeff has finished making a rope from his parachute cords, and he and Gloria start down to the lower ledge.

Wayne cuts the cords off his chute and yours, then kicks both chutes off the ledge. They slide down the icefield. He knots all the cords together, ties one rope end around his waist, and gives you the other end. He shows you how to anchor him. Taking out a hunting knife, he leans down and cuts two footholds in the ice. He steps into them. You pay out rope as Wayne cuts his way down the icefield. He has used up almost all the rope when he lets out a shout. You watch in horror as his body bounds down onto the rocks.

You shout, but there is no answer. Then you hear Jeff calling from the ledge. "Come on down," Jeff yells. "There's another ledge below this one."

"Wayne fell. I can't leave him," you shout back.

"You have to. He's had it," Jeff argues.

But supposing Wayne is only knocked out? you wonder. Anyway, he has the only knife. You think you can see it stuck into the ice near the dangling end of the rope. You'll need that knife for survival. But supposing you climb down, and Wayne is dead? Then what will you do?

Go on to PAGE 48.

You notice a slight movement in Wayne's body and decide to go down to him. You'll need the rope, so you pull it up and loop it over your shoulder. Facing into the ice-field, you cling to the slope and find a foot-hold with your right foot. Then you slide it lower, searching for the next cut-out step. You find it, then bring your left foot down into the first foothold. Despite the cold, sweat breaks out on your forehead. But you have made your first move! You are grateful for the good balance you learned as a gym-nast. Slowly you descend until finally you are at the spot from which Wayne fell. And there is the knife, sticking out of the ice. Somehow he must have got the rope snarled, then cut through the wrong strand, and fallen.

You can leave Wayne where he is, climb back up to the ledge, and try to follow Jeff and Gloria. Or you can drive the knife fur-ther into the ice, tie one end of the rope to the handle, and lower yourself to where Wayne is sprawled on the rocks below. Then you can retrieve the knife by yanking on the rope until the knife works loose and falls.

If you climb back up to follow Jeff and Gloria, turn to PAGE 54.

If you continue on down to Wayne, turn to PAGE 72.

You turn the key in the lock, push the door open, and crawl into a small room. After a while your eyes get used to the dark, and you notice two wooden chests in a corner. You go over and force the lids open. Even in the dark you can see the dazzle of gold! You run your hands through the coins. You are rich! There must be a million dollars' worth of gold coins in the two chests. Just wait till you tell the others!

But hold on a moment, you think. Why not keep all the gold for yourself? Finders keepers, right? All you have to do now is to stay where you are until night comes. When you don't return, they will think you are lost or dead and they will leave the fort. Anyway, you didn't like them very much. Why share your good fortune with them?

On the other hand, Pierre and Maria didn't do anything to hurt you. Pierre shared his M&M's with you and Maria, didn't he? Shouldn't they have a share in your good luck? After all, there is enough for everyone.

If you stay with the gold, turn to PAGE 52.

If you go back to your friends, turn to PAGE 56.

You stand between the rails and hold up your arms. There is no way the engineer can't see you. In fact, he blows his mournful whistle. *Hoooo-eeee! Hoooo-eeee!*

But the train doesn't slow down. You think of jumping to safety, but you want to make sure the engineer sees you, so you stand your ground. The light is still fifty yards away. Then you hear the squeal of brakes and see a stream of sparks shoot out from under the front wheels. Now you realize that the train is very close—too close!

With a yell, you jump. But before you clear the rails something hits you in the side, and you pass out.

When you come to, you are in the cab of the locomotive. The engineer and the fireman are watching you.

"You were lucky we have an old-fashioned cowcatcher on the front of the locomotive," the engineer says. "I never thought it would be a peoplecatcher someday. It scooped you up just in time."

He starts the locomotive, and soon you are speeding down the rails to

THE END

You let out a yell. To heck with the others, you are rich! Why should you share? Finders keepers, losers weepers. You will stay the night with your gold. In the morning you will return to the fort. By then Pierre and Maria will be gone.

You scoop gold coins out until both chests are empty. The coins are all shapes and sizes. Some are as big as a silver dollar, some the size of a penny. Most are round but some are square, and some even have a hole in the middle.

You lay face down on top of the coins. Lovely gold, all yours! You roll around in it, pour gold coins over your head. "Gold head!" you cry. You balance gold coins across the backs of your hands. "Gold fingers!" you shout. You let coins rain down on your chest. "Gold body!" you yell.

Then you get serious. You have to count all the coins to find out how many you have. You get busy and start counting and stacking. Hours pass. Night falls, and you stretch out and go to sleep.

In the middle of the night you hear a loud bang! What was that? Probably a stone falling into the well, you decide, and go back to sleep.

Go on to PAGE 53.

In the morning you get ready to leave. You notice then that the door is shut. You push against it, but it won't budge. A terrible feeling grips your heart. The bang in the middle of the night—it must have been a gust of wind slamming shut the door. Now it is locked, and the key is on the outside!

Wildly, you turn around. You still have your gold! You fling handfuls of coins against the door as though gold can do anything—even batter the door down.

"Help! Help!" you scream. "Get me out of here!"

Those neat piles of gold are now scattered all over the floor. You throw yourself down on top of all those shining coins and begin to whimper. "My gold, my gold," you moan. "Mine, all mine."

But no one hears you, no one is listening; and Time creeps by in his petty pace from day to endless day until

THE END

You pull the knife out of the ice and slip it into your belt. You check to make sure the rope is still securely looped over your shoulder, and you start climbing back up the icy rock face, using the cut-out holds. Several times you almost fall, but finally you manage to reach the ledge again. After a short rest, you shout down the other side to Jeff and Gloria. There is no answer.

You sit down. You have made a real mess of things. You should have gone with Jeff and Gloria in the first place. As your sister Cristina likes to say, "If there's a wrong way of doing something, you'll find it." You've found it, all right.

Sulking will get you nowhere, you realize, so you throw off your bad mood, tie one end of the rope around a rock knob near the edge of the ledge, and throw the other end down. It just reaches the lower ledge. You start down, hand over hand, the rope between your legs. You make it to the lower ledge and peer over. You see no one. You shout. No answer. Did you expect Jeff and Gloria to wait for you?

You notice it's a sheer fall of about fifty feet to a spike of rock. You wonder how Jeff and Gloria got down. It looks as if there's an easy slope not too far below. But to get down to the spike you need a rope, and yours is tied tightly to the upper ledge.

Go on to PAGE 55.

You can't pull it loose. You decide you will have to climb back up the rope, then go down the icefield to Wayne, after all. As you know, it's much harder to climb up a free-hanging rope than it seems, but it's your only chance. You get up about twenty feet before your strength runs out, and you slide back down again.

You try again and again, each time gaining less height as you tire more easily. Exhausted, you finally give up. You are trapped; you can go neither up nor down. Night falls, and you curl up on your rocky platform.

The next day you figure out a new way of getting down off the ledge. The rope is made from three strands braided together. Suppose you climbed as high as you could and cut the rope? You would then fall back to the ledge with at least fifteen feet of rope. You could unravel the strands, tie them end to end, and perhaps have enough to reach the lower spike of rock. But what would happen if a single strand of rope didn't hold you? Suppose the rope broke? You would fall to your death. Maybe it's better to wait on the ledge and hope that rescue planes fly by and spot you.

If you try to reach the lower ledge, turn to PAGE 68.

If you try waiting on the ledge, turn to PAGE 65.

You close the door and put the key in your pocket, then stand in the bottom of the well. The stone-lined walls are straight up and covered with moss. You start up, your back pressed against one wall and your feet jammed against the opposite wall. Halfway to the top, you slip and start to fall. You hit the bottom of the well with a cry of pain! You have cut your shin, and it is bleeding. You clap handfuls of moss on the wound. While you wait for the bleeding to stop, you shout up the well: "Help! Help!"

No one answers.

You try climbing again, and again you fall. You will never get out alive. You have found a fortune, but you'll never be able to spend it! You get angry then and attack the sides of the well one more time. This time, crying with pain and exhaustion, you make it to the top, roll your body away from the edge of the hole, and pass out.

An hour later you come to, stumble to your feet, and look for the others. As you draw near the fort, you spot a large tourist bus. What is this? Tourists are strolling around, taking photographs like crazy.

You find Pierre and ask, "What's going on?"

Go on to PAGE 57.

"A tourist bus stops here once a month," Pierre explains. "We are saved! We can return with them."

Maria laughs and gives you a big hug.

You listen to the tour guide, talking to the tourists. "There is an old legend that hundreds of years ago a pirate buried two chests of gold somewhere in the fort."

"Aah, that's all bunk!" a tourist says.

"You never know," the guide answers.

You whisper to Pierre. "Someday soon we three will return to this place."

"Me? Never!" Pierre says.

"Me neither," Maria agrees.

On the ride back to civilization, you tell them about the gold in the room in the bottom of the well. But Pierre and Maria don't believe you. They think your mind has been affected by the sun. So much the better, you decide. You will have all the gold for yourself, after all!

THE END

The train comes thundering on. You stand beside the tracks and wave, but it looks as if the engineer can't see you. You jump back and cry out, but the train roars on past — you count cars as they go by. You can't believe they have missed seeing you. *Twenty-five*, you count. There was a powerful headlight on the locomotive. Those dummies, you think. You shout and scream and throw handfuls of gravel against the side of the boxcars trundling by. Unfortunately, the train is going too fast for you to run alongside and try and hitch a ride. *Fifty*, you count. *Seventy*. You notice that the train seems to be slowing down. Maybe now you can run alongside, grab a handrail, and swing yourself up. *Eighty*, you count, and then spot the caboose.

With a shout of joy you realize that the train is slowing down even more! The long string of cars grinds and buckles to a stop. The caboose is just by you. The engineer did see you, after all! He wanted to stop when he knew you would be near the rear end of the train.

A brakeman carrying a lantern leads the way up into the caboose. Soon you are sitting on a box, warming your hands at a potbellied stove. The brakeman hands you a cup of coffee, and you start to tell him your story, right from the beginning to

THE END

After trying for hours to open the lock with the key, you give up. It's obviously rusted shut. There was probably nothing in there anyway, you decide. Much to your surprise, you find it easy to climb out of the well. Your body seems to weigh almost nothing. You wonder if you have lost that much weight. You head back to the others. After a while you wonder why you can't find them, or even catch any sight of the fort. Where did they go? How could everything have disappeared?

No matter where you look, all you see is desert brush. Then you discover something that chills the blood in your veins — an empty bottle! You pick it up. It's the same bottle, the one you found when you first entered the fort. What is going on? You couldn't have imagined that fort! Are you still at the bottom of the well, knocked out, or even? . . .

You remember how light you felt climbing up out of the well, as though you had no body. You pat yourself. *But I'm real,* you say to yourself. You whirl around. Everywhere you look, the shadows are long in the late afternoon sun. Everywhere — except one place.

Your body casts no shade!

THE END

You go back to Cliff and divide the food equally.

"Now what?" Cliff asks.

"Now we light a fire and hope the smoke will attract rescue planes," you say. You get busy and soon a big column of smoke is rising.

You hear a faint whirring sound.

"What's that?" Cliff asks.

"A helicopter!" you shout. It comes closer and closer, then hovers in the sky, about fifty feet up.

"We're saved!" Cliff screams.

"Not yet," you say. "The helicopter can't land because the ground is too steep."

Then a long steel cable comes snaking down from the belly of the craft. At the end of the line there are two big hooks facing opposite directions, like a giant double fish hook. It's used to rescue people off mountain ledges. No matter how the line goes down, there will always be one hook facing inward for the stranded person to grab.

You catch one hook, Cliff catches the other, and you are both reeled up into the body of the machine. Unfortunately, your rescuers turn out to be guerilla fighters who hold you and Cliff for ransom. And, unfortunately, no one comes forth to pay the ransom. The both of you spend the rest of your days on KP duty for the guerilla army.

THE END

Soon you, Pierre, and Maria stop and make another shelter with your parachute. In digging away the sand to anchor one end of the chute, you discover that the ground is much cooler down a foot or so. You tell the others to dig shallow graves and cover themselves with sand. You do the same.

You try to sleep. Hours pass. You hear a curious snuffling noise. You look out. There, twenty yards away, a desert cougar is looking in at you!

"What should we do?" you whisper.

Maria shakes her head and whispers back, "Nothing."

"What can we do?" Pierre asks.

You are scared out of your wits. If you had your dog Flash with you, he'd soon scare the cougar away. But you don't have Flash; you'll have to scare the animal away yourself.

"He will kill somebody if we don't act," Pierre says. "Let's all jump up at the same time and scream. Maybe it will frighten him away."

The animal doesn't look very scared as he licks his chops. His long tail twitches from side to side, and he advances yet another step toward you.

If you think you should all jump up and scream, turn to PAGE 64.

If you think you should all play dead, turn to PAGE 69.

"Follow me!" General Killmore waves his arm as though he were waving a sword. Everyone falls into line. As you hike along, you talk to Jenny Jogalotto. Although she looks at least sixty, she moves like a person half that age.

"You're in terrific shape," you tell her.

"I'm seventy-two and I just ran a marathon in Peru," she says. "That's twenty-six miles, nonstop."

"Wow, that's great!"

"I hold the world record in the mile for seventy-year-olds," Jenny says. "I can outrun any seventy-year-old anywhere, and most sixty- and fifty-year-olds, too. Man or woman, makes no difference." She stops, catches your arm, and says, "Wait a minute. Let's split. I can't stand traveling with these slowpokes. You're young and able to keep up with me."

She does seem a lot more fit than the others. On the other hand, you would feel more secure with three or four people instead of just one.

You hesitate.

"Well, are you coming or not?" Jenny demands.

You decide to rejoin the group on PAGE 67.

Before you go, you *watch* Jenny jog off on her own. "Good luck," you call to her.

"Okay, on the count of three we all jump up," you tell Pierre and Maria.

"One!" you call.

The cougar twitches his tail.

"Two!" you cry.

The cougar crouches down.

"Three!"

You all jump up and scream like crazy.

The cougar springs.

Crunch! (Pierre.)

The cougar springs again.

Crunch! (Maria.)

The cougar springs for the third time.

Crunch! (You-know-who.)

Sorry about that.

THE END

You pass another night on the ledge, and the next day you try once again to climb the rope. You fail and fall back to the ledge, exhausted. A plane passes by overhead, and you jump up and down and wave, but it flies on and out of sight.

That evening you eat the leather strap on your wristwatch. The next morning you lick the dew off all the rocks you can reach from your ledge. Your lips are cracked and bleeding, but you're so thirsty you don't care. Soon you cut the tongues out of your leather boots and eat them. That only makes your thirst worse.

The next day you are so weak you can hardly move around. You crawl up against a rock and huddle there. Is this the end? Will you ever see home again? You can't believe how cold it is. You're very tired, but you don't dare go to sleep — you might freeze to death. You fight sleep, but eventually your eyes close.

That night it snows heavily. In the morning you are only a white bump on the ledge, just another big rock covered with snow.

Go on the PAGE 66.

One day, five years later, a scientist comes to the foot of the mountain. He is trying to capture a rare butterfly. The butterfly scoots up just out of reach of his net. At that moment, a shower of white bones falls down the cliff face. The scientist picks up a small bone and turns it this way and that, looking at its delicate features.

"Bird bone, it looks like," he says. He puts it away in his collecting sack and adds, "From an eagle's wing, probably."

For the next fifty years the scientist keeps your wrist bone on his desk until he, too, in his turn, becomes a collection of bones.

THE END

As you walk along with the group, Dr. Drib asks, "Where is Jenny?"

"She split," you say. "She wanted me to go with her, but I wouldn't."

The General waves his arm. "Keep up, men."

"Frankly, I think the General is a little nuts," Spike Harris says.

"Maybe the crash affected his mind," you say.

"I know one thing," Spike says. "I'll never show him my map."

What map? you wonder. This is the first you've heard that someone has a map.

The trail leads into a swamp. The General stops and holds up his arms. "This could lead to an ambush," he says. He kneels down and puts an ear to the ground. "No tanks coming! The ground isn't shaking. Forwaaaaaaard!"

Suddenly you hear a high-pitched whistle from the swamp.

"That's the Double Mop Meetu Dipper!" Dr. Drib shouts. "I must find it!"

"Somebody better follow him and bring him back," you argue. "He'll only get lost."

Should you go after Dr. Drib or not?

Quick, think of the names of birds. If you can think of six birds, fly to PAGE 70.

If you don't know the difference between a crow and an ostrich, hop to PAGE 75.

68

You climb up the rope, cut it, and fall back to the ledge. Fortunately, you are not hurt. You untie the strands, join them end to end, and tie one end of your makeshift rope around a rock knob. Then you start down the thin rope, hoping it won't break. Your heart is in your mouth as you drop the last few feet and grab the rocky spike. *Whew!* Luck is with you. Now, if you are careful, you can climb safely down to the easy rocky slope.

You reach it. There is no sign of Jeff and Gloria, but hours later, sweaty and worn out, you run across footprints on a trail at the bottom of the mountain. It must be they, you decide. You follow the prints and . . .

Flip back to the bottom of PAGE 16.

You lie very still, your eyes shut. The cougar comes closer. You can hear his heavy breathing. His hot breath smells like old gym sneakers. Something wet and rough scrapes across your face. He is licking the salt in your sweat! You are ready to scream, but the licking stops. Your heart is pounding. You can't take much more of this. You hear a soft noise in the sand. Your eyes flicker open.

"He's gone," Pierre whispers.

You squirm out of your shallow grave. You find the cougar's tracks, and cautiously follow him. You spot him again. He is sitting down beside an animal he has killed and half-eaten. It looks like a wild goat. Now you know why he wasn't hungry when he entered your shelter. You think of scaring him away from his kill. Even raw, the goat meat will provide food and moisture. You pick up a stick. Should you wait him out until he leaves the goat meat and wanders off? Or should you shout, then jump forward with the stick to see if it frightens him?

Give a good loud shout. If anyone answers, turn to PAGE 74.

If no one answers your shout, turn to PAGE 77.

You run into the swamp and catch up with Dr. Drib.

"You want to see the DMMD, too?" he asks.

"The DMMD?"

"The Double Mop Meetu Dipper," he says.

"Actually, I think the General is nuts. That's why I left him," you admit.

"A wonderful man," Dr. Drib says. "Someday his picture will be on a postage stamp or a cereal box."

"Are you coming back?" you ask.

"No. Ssssh!" He puts one finger to his lips. "Hear that?"

All you hear is a series of long and short bird whistles.

"That bird is talking nonsense," Dr. Drib says.

"The bird's talking?" you repeat.

"Yes. Its calls are always in Morse code, but it never makes any sense."

You whistle SOS in Morse code: three longs, three shorts, three longs.

A repeat of your message comes out of the swamp. To make sure, you whistle the SOS again. Again the bird whistles back: three longs, three shorts, three longs.

"It's finally making sense," Dr. Drib says.

"If I solve the mystery," you say, "will you come back with me to the others?"

Go on to PAGE 71.

"It's a deal," he agrees.

"Okay, here's what I think. Somehow the bird picks up Morse code from passing planes or ships at sea. It repeats the message it hears — the Morse code — only backward. Say it hears the word *west* in Morse code. It repeats the last letter first, then *s*, *e*, and *w*. That's why its calls never make sense."

"But it made sense repeating your SOS," Dr. Drib says.

"That's because SOS is the same backward or forward," you say.

"You're a genius!" Dr. Drib says.

"You gave me the idea," you admit.

"Me? How?"

"The DMMD. It's the same backward and forward."

"So it is! Congratulations, you have solved a great puzzle in the bird world. I'm going to name the new room in our Museum of Odd Birds after you."

"Thanks a lot," you say. "Okay, let's get back to the others."

As you hike along, you keep thinking there is something odd about Dr. Drib's name. What is it?

Then, as you leave the swamp, there comes a final burst of Morse code, a final good-bye from the DMMD bird. The dots and dashes spell out two words —

EHT DNE

You decide to make your way down to Wayne. You bang the knife into the ice all the way up to the hilt and tie the rope to the handle. You kick yourself down, hand-under-hand on the rope. You are sweating with fear. Will the rope hold? Will the knife stay in the ice? You will soon find out.

You are only ten feet from the bottom when the knife starts to pull out. Your stomach drops. At the last second you spot one of the discarded chutes, and with an acrobatic leap, you land on top of it and roll over. You find the knife, then go over to Wayne. His eyes are closed, but he is still breathing. There is no blood anywhere, and nothing seems to be broken.

You cut a piece of ice and hold it to his forehead. After a while he comes to. For a moment he is still dazed. Then he sits up and buttons the top of his shirt. "Why did you open my shirt?" he demands. "Were you searching me?"

"No, I wanted to make sure that nothing was choking you," you say, puzzled by his question. You notice he wears several jewelry chains around his neck. On one of them there is a good luck charm, a gold four-leaf clover.

Go on to PAGE 73.

"Can you walk?" you ask. Perhaps, if he's not too badly hurt, he can lean on you as he walks along. The important thing is to get out into the open somewhere where you can light a fire and perhaps be spotted by a rescue plane.

Wayne stands up and tries to walk, but then sits down again with a cry of pain. "You'll have to hike out for help," he says. "I saw a river. Maybe you can reach that."

"I can't leave you. You're hurt too badly. How can you survive without food or water?" you ask.

"You go along and save yourself," he says. "I'll manage."

He isn't making sense, you realize. Perhaps the fall has affected his head.

"Tell you what, we'll stay for the rest of the day," you say. "If we hear a plane between now and nightfall, it means search planes are looking for us, so we'll stay here for a couple of days. We can lay out a signal with strips of parachute cloth. If no plane comes before nightfall, we'll hike out together first thing in the morning. Maybe you'll feel better by then."

If you have seen or heard an airplane today, turn to PAGE 79.

If you haven't seen or heard an airplane today, turn to PAGE 84.

You jump up, shout, and wave the stick. The cougar springs. One whop of his paw, and you go flying head over heels. You stagger to your feet and run, the animal close on your heels. But the cougar doesn't want to leave his kill, and he soon stops. However, he is now between you and Pierre and Maria. You try to sneak past him, but he moves to cut you off. Pierre and Maria run off and disappear.

You sit cross-legged on the ground. The cougar sits down opposite you, twenty yards away. It is a stalemate.

You stare at the cougar.

The cougar stares back.

Night falls, and you can see his big, yellow, unblinking eyes in the darkness. He can see your bright, feverish eyes staring back at him.

Morning comes, and still you stare at each other.

On April 1, 1999, Captain Juan Soto of the South American Army finds two skeletons in the desert. He writes in his official report: "I found the two skeletons twenty yards apart, facing each other. The human skeleton was sitting cross-legged. The cougar skeleton was in a crouched position. It almost seems as if human and beast had stared each other to death."

THE END

Dr. Drib disappears into the swamp. Now only you, the General, and Spike Harris are left. After several hours of hiking, you suggest a rest.

"Fine," the General agrees. "But one man stays awake while the others sleep, in case of hostiles."

"Hostiles?" you ask.

"People who might attack us," the General explains.

Sometime later the General wakes you both. He is pointing to a line of trees in the distance. "Do you see them?" he asks.

At first you don't see anything. Then you notice the heads of two people. They seem to be gliding from the protection of one tree to the next.

"They are trying to outflank us," the General says.

"Outflank us?" you repeat.

"Sneak around behind us," the General explains. "I have noticed they always move from right to left. Obviously there is a column of them somewhere, and they are sneaking by our position, two or three at a time, under cover of the trees. Old eagle eyes here misses nothing."

"But who are they?" you ask. "Natives?"

"Who cares?" the General says. "They are hostiles. They must be dealt with."

Go on to PAGE 76.

"Why don't we run away and hide?" Spike asks.

"Hide? Nonsense, we will attack!"

"Attack with what?" Spike asks. "We have no arms."

"We have courage," the General says. "Come. I will lead you into battle and turn you into heroes!"

"I'm getting out of here," Spike says.

The General thrusts his arm out, as though he were waving a sword. "Forward! Victory is ours!" He breaks into a trot.

The valley rings with the General's cries. The ground shakes under the thunder of his boots. The birds fall silent. The hostiles wait.

"That idiot will get us killed," Spike says. "I'm splitting!"

You realize that Spike is right. The General definitely doesn't have all his marbles. The safest thing to do is go with Spike and leave the General behind. But you've grown to like the General. Somehow things are always exciting when he is around. And how can you run away and hurt his feelings? He obviously thinks you are right behind him.

If you have seen a war movie in the past week, turn to PAGE 85.

If you haven't seen a war movie, turn to PAGE 82.

You were smart to wait. The cougar wanders off. Unfortunately, he finished off the goat.

Pierre shows up, all excited. "Come on," he says, all excited. "The river is not far away."

You join him and Maria.

"I saw a bunch of long-necked birds fly past, heading south," Pierre says. "I am sure they are river birds."

It takes you most of the day, but finally you come in sight of the river. You all rush down the bank and into the water. When you have drunk your fill, you then agree to head downriver. After a while you notice that the land is turning swampy.

"I think we should turn back," Pierre says.

You spot some smoke downriver. "Look," you say. "Where there's a fire, there're bound to be people, right?"

You press ahead in swampy water up to your ankles. The going gets squashier and squashier. The water level is soon at your knees. Pierre, afraid of quicksand, complains that he is sinking.

"Let's go back," Maria says.

"But we're almost there," you argue.

Go on to PAGE 78.

Ahead of you there is an island of some sort in the swamp. You can see huts and natives. But now the water is up to your chest. You step forward and sink completely under water. When you come up, you shout for help. A grass rope lands beside you. You grab it, and some natives haul you up on the island. Just in time.

They haul Pierre and Maria up, too. The natives feed and take care of you. They teach you how to fish, how to make huts, and how to build canoes out of reeds.

When their village gets too dirty, these swamp people simply move to another island in the swamp and make new huts. Then they go back and burn their old village in a big holiday called Cleaning Up Your Room Day. On that day they cook up a big feast and hold sing-songs.

You know you will be rescued eventually, but you aren't in a hurry. You are having too good a time fishing, making reed boats, floating around from one island to another, and hanging out at the local witch doctor's hut. You don't care if you are ever rescued!

THE END

That evening you and Wayne hear a plane. Someone must be out searching for you! The next day you cut one of the chutes into long strips. In a clear space, you lay out the strips to form a huge letter H for *help!*

Sure enough, a plane appears and roars just over your heads. The craft soars into the sky, then lets out a stream of white smoke. Is something wrong with his engine? No, he is skywriting!

You and Wayne anxiously spell out the letters the pilot has written. H E L L O.

"He thinks our H means *hello*," Wayne says.

You both jump up and down to attract the pilot's attention. Then you swiftly change the strips of parachute cloth to form a huge letter L for *land*.

The pilot makes another low pass, then starts climbing. Soon big white letters start to appear.

"*Move?*" Wayne asks.

"No, it's *love*," you say. "See?"

Now the letters are easy to make out. L O V E. Then two more signs appear: a U and a 2.

"Love you, too," Wayne says with disgust.

Go on to PAGE 80.

You slap your forehead. "That dummy! He thinks our L means *love*."

"Now what do we do?" Wayne asks.

"How about a C for *crash* or a J for *jump*?" you suggest.

"Or a D D for *drop dead*?" Wayne says. "Now what is he doing?"

The pilot is making a long bar. He cuts the smoke, flies a big curve, and comes back to the head of the bar. Two fast passes, two short strokes, and an arrow appears. It points south.

"He must want us to go that way," you say.

"Maybe there is a rescue party in that direction," Wayne says.

You decide to follow the arrow. After an hour the plane flies over again and writes out a final message in huge white letters.

This is the message:

When it gets dark you and Gloria shelter as best you can in your rough lean-to. In the morning Gloria's ankle feels better. You cut a walking stick for her, and you both set out, hoping to catch up with Jeff.

You follow a rough trail you think Jeff may have taken. Finally it grows dark, and you have to stop. You find shelter under some bushes on the bank of a tiny stream. The next morning Gloria's ankle is all swollen again, and there is no way she can walk on it.

You are both just sitting there, feeling sorry for yourselves, when Gloria says, "You know what? We'll never get out of this mess."

"Something will turn up," you say. "We have to trust the author."

"That dope?" Gloria says. "I bet he's completely out of fresh beginnings."

Gloria is right. This is

THE END

You trot after the General, who is just entering the row of trees. The General stops. Are the hostiles attacking?

"Wait! I'm coming," you shout.

As you reach the General, you see a river in front of you that was hidden by the line of trees growing on its bank. Now you realize that the so-called hostiles, who seemed to be gliding from tree to tree, were actually floating down the river in canoes and rafts.

"No battle?" the General says, looking disappointed.

"Cheer up," you tell him. "I think we're about to be rescued." You point to a raft with two men on it coming down the river.

"Ahoy!" you shout. "Take us on board!"

The men shout back that the current is too strong for them to put in to shore.

"We'll have to swim for it," you tell the General. You both plunge into the river and manage to reach the raft, where the two men help you up. Their names are Huck and Jim. They share their food with you, but they are rather weird characters. They keep pretending to be pirates, or a slave trader and his slave, or Arab chieftains.

"I think they're spies," the General whispers to you. "Let's unmask them."

Go on to PAGE 83.

Fortunately, just then the raft makes it to a sawmill. You thank the two men for their help. "Who are you?" you ask Huck and Jim. "Where did you come from?"

"We're straight out of a book," Huck says, giving Jim a big grin.

All the way back to civilization you think of your rescuers. Who did they remind you of? Then you remember the famous story and the name of the book. You will have to read it and start out on a new adventure with Huck and Jim, even though *this* adventure has come to

THE END

No plane appears that day. Next morning you and Wayne start hiking out. At midday you enter a forest. You spot a path. Maybe you're getting closer to civilization. You follow the path until it reaches a stream. On the other side of the stream, the trail seems to lead deeper into the jungle. "We have to make a decision about following that trail," you say.

"The trail could lead us somewhere," Wayne points out. "If we find natives, they might help us."

"But if we follow the stream, it should lead to a river," you say. "And the river is bound to lead to civilization."

"You want to face all kinds of poisonous fish and snakes?" Wayne asks.

"And how about the dangerous animals and snakes on the jungle trail?" you counter.

"Why don't you follow the river, and I'll follow the path?" Wayne suggests.

"That's crazy!" you say. "Why split up? It only lessens our chances."

"It doubles our chances," Wayne argues. "If either of us makes it out, he can send help back to the other."

Your feelings are hurt. After all you have done to help Wayne, now he wants to split.

If you can swim, follow the stream and turn to PAGE 86.

If you can't swim, stay with Wayne and turn to PAGE 91.

You catch up with Spike and say, "Tell me about this map of yours."

"It's a map of a Spanish ship that was carrying gold from Peru when it went down in a hurricane," Spike says. "I found the ship and was on my way back to get money for a salvage operation when the plane crashed."

"Is there much treasure?" you ask.

"Millions," Spike says, "and I'm going to need someone young and strong like you to go back for the treasure when we get out of here."

You notice the land is changing, becoming more junglelike, with thorny brush and thick vines everywhere around you. "Let's climb up into the trees and swing along from vine to vine," you suggest, forgetting about the treasure.

You both climb up. Long, hanging vines make it easy to travel through the trees. Finally you come to a clearing. You climb down and cautiously enter the area.

Three trails lead out of the clearing: to the south, to the east, and to the west.

If you're lefthanded, take the west trail and turn to PAGE 89.

If you're righthanded, take the east trail and turn to PAGE 93.

If you're ambidextrous (use both hands equally well), take the south trail and turn to PAGE 90.

You wave good-bye to Wayne, who takes the trail into the jungle. Ignoring the possibility of piranha fish and poisonous snakes, you wade into the stream. You trip on hidden roots. Hanging thorns scratch your face.

Hours later you are standing downstream, taking a brief rest, when a weighted net comes sailing out of the shadows and drops over your head. You struggle and find yourself being dragged up on the bank. Strange-looking, near-naked men dance around you, shaking their spears.

This is it, you think, they will kill you. But to your surprise, they free you from the net. Then the leader pokes you in the chest and says, "*Genotto? Goniffle?*"

"Same to you," you say.

He shouts, "*Goykopele!*" The others roar and shake spears at you.

You notice that all their words start with a *hard* G sound, so you desperately think of *hard* G words.

"Give! Go! Get!" you yell. "Golly! Gum!"

Suddenly, they throw down their spears, rush into the river, and wash their necks.

"Great!" you shout. "Good guys!"

Next they all come rushing out of the stream, their cheeks puffed out. They line up in a circle, each man's hands on the shoulders of the man in front.

Go on to PAGE 88.

"Gargle gollywogs! Godzilla's goose!" you cry, just to keep the conversation going.

Suddenly each man is trying to spurt a stream of water into the ear of the man in front of him.

Now if you can figure out which words made them do what, everything would be gunky-gory, as they probably say. Later you learn that the Gackadaze, as the natives are called, were just doing their usual noontime Water-Shoot-Ear ceremony.

You stay with the Gackadaze and learn Gench, their language. You also learn how to make a deadly poison from the spines of the *killi-killi* fish and how to train a hummingbird to fly upside down. In return, you teach the Gackadaze how to whistle through their fingers and how to rub their bellies and pat their heads at the same time.

Years pass and you become an elder in the tribe. One day, in the year 2020, an expedition finds you. You say good-bye to your Gackadaze friends and return home where you are hailed as the Rip Van Winkle of the twenty-first century! You give talks at schools and meet the President. Everything is great, except that once in a while you forget yourself near water fountains and do the Gackadaze Water-Shoot-Ear ceremony. However, your friends soon learn to wear earmuffs when they're around you.

THE END

You and Spike take the trail to the west. In late afternoon you come across a frightening sight. Three men are buried up to their necks in the middle of a clearing.

"Look!" Spike says. On the opposite side of the clearing three horsemen are wheeling around on their mounts.

The horsemen line up and suddenly the three horses are galloping toward the three heads! Each horseman is holding a lance in the charge position.

"They're going to kill those men!" you cry out. "Come on!"

You both run toward the unfortunate prisoners and manage to reach the buried captives just before the horses get there.

A curious wheeled cart comes whizzing along. On it a man sits behind a movie camera.

"Fools! You have ruined my scene!" he shouts. "You are messing up my movie!"

You look over and see a makeup man carefully combing the hair of one of the buried prisoners. Finally, you and Spike are forgiven for interrupting the movie. In fact, the boss of the company wants to make a film of Spike going after his treasure. The movie director even offers you a part. It is going to be an exciting year for you. You are going to search for lost treasure, and you're going to be a movie star!

THE END

You and Spike follow the southbound trail and come to an open field where you sit down to rest. For a moment you close your eyes. After a while you notice people working in a field. Why, it's a rubber band farm! You join them and are given food and water. Then you are asked to pick rubber bands that grow on low bushes. You have to turn over the leaves, then snatch the bands before the sun makes them too sticky to pull off.

Everyone in the nearby village works on rubber bands. The next day you go to work in the packing sheds. Your job is to sort out the bands according to size: huge, average, or teensies. Teensies barely go around your little finger.

You visit Spike in the testing shed. He stands in a big pile of broken rubber bands, wringing his hands. "Too much! Too much tension!" he cries.

"Let's get out of here," you say.

Suddenly you are slammed into a huge rubber strap that goes around your waist. Giant mechanical arms pull the strap tight.

Twaaannnnnnng! You are shot off like a paper clip!

You scream and wake up. You fell asleep and had a nightmare. Get up, go back to the bottom of PAGE 85, and choose either the east or west trail.

You and Wayne hike all day. Just before dark you come to a clearing where two people are crouched over a fire.

"Sssssh!" Wayne warns you.

You hear a word or two of English and run forward to meet two passengers from the plane. You greet them joyfully. One is Captain Mundo of the Inter-American police. The other is Nadia Tocabien.

"All the passengers who stayed on the plane survived," says Captain Mundo. "But some were hurt and couldn't be moved. Nadia and I left to get help."

You tell them of your adventures, and Captain Mundo piles wood on the fire. "I was tipped off that a notorious diamond smuggler was on our flight," Captain Mundo explains. "However, I had nothing to go on."

"Do you think we'll be rescued soon?" Nadia asks.

"Sure," Wayne says. He places his hand on his heart. "I have what it takes to save myself."

"You mean courage?" Nadia asks.

"Or your good luck charm?" Captain Mundo asks.

Just then a squad of soldiers arrives. They have been searching for survivors and spotted your campfire smoke. They tie up their horses and stay for the night.

Go on to PAGE 92.

That night you lie beside the fire and remember how angry Wayne was that you had searched him when he was knocked out. You remember that he seemed to be badly hurt, until he realized that you were not going to leave him. Then he quickly got better. You remember how he always seemed to want to be on his own. Other clues fall into place, and as you drift off to sleep, you think what a big surprise you will have for everyone in the morning.

After breakfast, you point to Wayne and tell Captain Mundo, "There's your diamond smuggler. Arrest him!"

"You're crazy!" Wayne shouts.

"Look at some of those chains around his neck. I bet you find a small bag of diamonds hanging from one of them."

The captain searches Wayne and finds the diamonds.

"But how did you know?" Captain Mundo asks.

"He said he had what it takes to save himself and put his hand on his chest. He was really talking about the diamonds." You also tell him the other clues that led you to suspect Wayne.

"You'll get a reward for this," Captain Mundo says.

You return home a hero!

THE END

You and Spike follow the east trail. Toward evening you spot a cave in a hillside. Spike wants to check it out. You both crawl into the cave and hear the sound of running water. You are thirsty, but the cave is pitch-black, and you have to crawl. You both keep talking, so that you won't lose each other. Finally you come to a huge cavern, the floor of which is an underground lake. You notice a dugout canoe that sits at a rocky landing.

"Let's paddle around," Spike suggests. "Maybe there's another way out."

"There must be, or it wouldn't be so light in here," you say.

Together you explore the underground room. "Look!" you point. "There's a tunnel leading out."

You glide into the tunnel. It gets darker and darker until finally it's pitch-black. Suddenly you break into a well-lit room. On a platform a business executive is seated at a desk. The person takes papers from one tray and puts them into another. Then you notice a nameplate on the desk. It has your name inscribed on it.

Go on to PAGE 94.

You glide out of that room and come into another room. Here the platform contains the inside of a spaceship. Two people are at the controls, their backs to you. One flight suit bears your name, the other suit Spike's name.

You glide on out and enter a third room. Now the platform is an operating room in a hospital. A masked surgeon is bending over someone on a table. The surgical gown has your name on the back. You enter still more rooms. Six? Eight? You lose track, but you realize that all these rooms are showing you different futures — different things that could happen in your later life.

Finally you leave the last room, and the dugout canoe tilts forward. You grab the sides. You are on a water ride!

Whooossssssh! You fly down the wooden sides of the flume.

At the bottom a group of people are cheering and clapping. They are all the survivors of *Crash Landing!* You recognize Wayne, Gloria, Jeff, Pierre, Maria, Jenny, Spike, Cliff, the General — all the people who have shared your adventure — which has now, finally (no kidding!), reached

THE END